Victor,
the Reluctant Vulture

by Jonathan Hanson

Illustrations by Kim Kanoa Duffek

Arizona-Sonora Desert Museum Press

For Bethany, in the hope that, like Victor,
you grow up to be happy with who you are.

JH ~ Tucson, Arizona

First Edition, English
Published in the United States of America by the
Arizona-Sonora Desert Museum
2021 N. Kinney Road, Tucson, Arizona 85743
www.desertmuseum.org

A Spanish edition of this book is also available. For more
information contact the ASDM Press.

This book is available at quantity discounts for educational,
business, or sales promotional use. For more information,
please contact: Arizona-Sonora Desert Museum Press
520-883-3028 | asdmpress@desertmuseum.org

ISBN 978-886679-45-0
Copyright registered with the U.S. Library of Congress

Book development and design by Linda M. Brewer
Printed in Canada by Friesens Corporation
Printed on paper from responsible sources and
made with 10% post-consumer waste

Contents

Victor's first memory, after he valiantly pushed his way out of the speckled egg his mother had laid nearly a month before, was of her featherless, bald red face barfing up half-digested slimy lumps of stuff, which she apparently expected him to eat.

This seemed just plain wrong to Victor, not to mention gross. And it smelled *terrible*. So he turned up his nose, or rather his beak, at the disgusting stuff, and let his hatch-mate, Vinnie, eat it all, which he seemed to do with relish. *Yuck.*

But soon Victor was weak from hunger, while Vinnie seemed to grow bigger and stronger by the hour. On the second morning after they had both hatched, Vinnie nearly shoved Victor right off the nest ledge trying to gobble up all the stuff Mother had deposited. So Victor gritted his teeth, or rather his beak, and began forcing down the slimy lumps, even though they tasted like, well, something that had been dead for a while, then eaten and barfed back up, to be honest. After that Victor began to grow quickly, but he would always be smaller and weaker than Vinnie.

"That's okay," his father, Vern, said when Victor worried about it. "Vultures don't need to be strong."

What's that supposed to mean? Victor wondered. After all, his Uncle Vlad (who often read old *National Geographic* magazines

4

he found in the landfill a few miles away) had told him vultures were *raptors*, members of a group of birds that included strong and swift hunters like hawks, owls, falcons, and even eagles. Raptors were definitely the coolest birds in the world, and Victor was proud to be one.

Early one day, while sitting in the nest practicing flapping his wings, Victor watched a Red-tailed Hawk swoop down from the sky and catch a rabbit fleeing at full speed through the desert. It was the most exciting thing Victor had ever seen, and he could hardly wait to try it. But didn't you need to be strong to chase down rabbits and rodents and quail and other prey?

"Boy, are *you* stupid," said Vinnie. Mother whacked Vinnie with her wing, and said to Victor, "You'll understand when you can fly and the flock teaches you how to find food. And don't believe everything your Uncle Vlad tells you." On nearby rock outcroppings, other vultures in the flock nodded their bald red heads in agreement. (Mother had a habit of saying, "It takes a flock to raise a fledgling.")

So Victor flapped his wings daily to strengthen them, forced down Mother's and Father's regurgitated meals, and waited for the day he could take off and soar into the distance, as he watched the adult vultures do every morning.

One afternoon Victor watched a group of four beautiful dark hawks with coppery shoulders and brilliant white bands on their tails. They were hunting a rabbit by taking turns swooping down at it to keep it from getting away. When they caught it, all of them got to eat part of it. Mother told Victor, after she came home and barfed, that these were Harris's Hawks, which were famous for hunting in family groups that included the young from the previous year. The young birds stayed with their parents to help raise the new hatchlings. "It's called *cooperative breeding*," Father said. "The young birds get more practice, which helps them be more successful when they head out on their own, and the parents benefit from the extra help in hunting."

Well, that sounded smart, and then it hit Victor: Maybe vultures were cooperative breeders, too, and maybe they hunted together and *that's* why they didn't need to be strong!

"Boy, are you *stupid*," said Vinnie, when Victor voiced his theory.

By this time, several weeks after they had hatched, Vinnie had almost all his adult feathers. And when he stood on the edge of the nest and flapped vigorously, his feet would sometimes rise several inches into the air. One morning, while the other flock members sat on nearby rocks and saguaro cactuses cheering him on, Vinnie took a huge breath and leaped off the nest flapping like crazy. While Victor watched in horror, Vinnie plunged straight down! But at the last second his wings caught the air, and he swooped upward again, Mother at his side shouting proud encouragement. The other flock members took off, and before Victor knew it they had all soared out of sight, and he was left entirely alone.

Victor spent all that day flapping as hard as he could, but only once did his

feet come off the nest. In the late afternoon he saw dark specks in the distant sky. It was the flock circling toward home, and soon they came gliding in one by one to flare their wings and land gracefully on rocks—all except for Vinnie, who overshot his approach and slammed into Victor, almost sending them both over the edge. "Sorry!" said Vinnie, grinning, and Victor saw that his mouth, or rather his beak, was stained. He had eaten something fresh! Vinnie saw his look, and said, "Jackrabbit!" with relish. Vinnie's first day hunting had been a success!

Darn it! thought Victor. *That's not fair!* Meanwhile Mother retched up some slimy pieces of already-eaten jackrabbit for him.

The next day Victor again practiced flapping as hard as he could, and by the time the flock came home he too was lifting off the nest without any trouble. This time Vinnie belched loudly after making a pretty decent landing, and said, "Venison today!"

"You guys killed a *deer*?" said Victor, astonished. He was beginning to think vultures might be the greatest hunters of all the raptors!

Vinnie just stared at him. "*Boy*, are you stupid!"

The next morning when Victor woke up and stretched his wings, he suddenly realized all the members of the flock were gathered around on nearby rocks and saguaros, and they were all watching *him*.

"Time for you to fly, Victor!" said Father.

Gulp. Victor slowly walked to the edge of the nest ledge. Funny. He had never thought about it before, but suddenly the drop to the ground below looked awfully far.

"C'mon, Victor, you can do it!" yelled his cousin Viggo.

Victor unfolded his wings and took a few tentative flaps. To tell the truth, he was terrified, and only the thought of yet another regurgitated meal kept him from chickening out. He inched forward until he was teetering at the edge of that huge drop. Then Victor took a big breath and flung himself off the nest into space, flapping like mad! To his surprise, he didn't plunge earthward like Vinnie had, but instead arced downward and then back upward in a graceful curve, with the flock by his side shouting encouragement.

"The kid's a natural!" yelled Uncle Vlad.

Indeed, Victor quickly found he could alter his course and speed and altitude by slightly tilting his wings and twisting his tail. Within minutes it seemed like the most natural thing in the world to be soaring high above the ground on nothing but a cushion of air.

"Wooooohooooooo!" he shouted.

"All right, Victor!" said Vinnie, coming up on his right. "Let's go find some *food*!"

"Sounds good to me!" said Victor.

The vulture flock—all 17 of them now—began circling in a thermal, getting higher and higher without even flapping their wings. Father explained it to him. "A thermal is a column of hot air above a spot on the ground that absorbs extra heat from the sun, or above the slope of a mountain. Since hot air rises, it creates an updraft that we can catch under our outstretched wings and lifts us high above the desert."

Higher and higher the vultures circled, until they were hundreds of feet above the ground. It was exhilarating, but Victor had one thing on his mind: Hunting! Vultures have superb vision, and Victor found he could make out tiny details on the ground, like for example that rabbit hopping between two bushes. Hey! A *rabbit*!

"HEY EVERYONE! THERE'S A RABBIT!" Victor shouted.

A chorus of "Where?" came from the flock.

"I don't smell anything," said Uncle Vlad, frowning.

"Me either," said Viggo.

"RIGHT *THERE*!" yelled Victor, almost beside himself. "HOPPING BETWEEN THOSE BUSHES!"

There was a long moment of silence while the flock members looked at each other uncomfortably.

"Uh . . . *hopping*?" said Uncle Vlad.

Suddenly Victor's mother was beside him. "Victor, dear, would you follow me, please?" she said. The two banked away from the flock, and Mother led him to another thermal, where they were able to circle each other within easy talking distance without flapping.

"Victor," Mother began, looking very earnest and concerned. "Vultures don't hunt live prey. We have a much more important role in nature."

Victor was totally confused by that. "I don't understand, Mother. What do you mean? We're raptors, aren't we? Like eagles and hawks and falcons?"

"Well, I'm not sure, dear. Some people have called us raptors. But hawks and falcons and eagles are birds of prey—they hunt animals like rabbits, which helps keep the rabbit population under control so a lot of rabbits don't starve or die of disease. And vultures don't hunt. We only eat carrion. We clean up what's left when a hawk kills a rabbit but doesn't eat it all, or when a pack of coyotes kills a deer, or when an animal dies of disease or old age. We also clean up the remains of the poor animals that get hit by cars and trucks on the roads. It's a very important niche."

Victor was so stunned by this statement that he didn't even wonder what "niche" meant. But the meaning of "carrion" was becoming only too clear.

"You mean . . ." he began, starting to tremble, "we only eat things that are *already dead*?"

"That's right, Victor. In fact, vultures are among the very few bird species that have a good sense of smell. The longer something's been dead"—and here Victor could have sworn she actually sounded *proud*—"the easier we can find it!"

"You mean when it's stinking and ROTTEN!" Victor yelled, growing more and more horrified.

Mother said primly, "Well, as a matter of fact, we eat freshly killed food when we can, but that's not always possible. And we don't think of it as "rotten"— we think of it as *aged*. Putrefaction releases a complex bouquet of aromas with surprisingly delicate overtones, if you pay attention. Hmph." Mother seemed to be a bit miffed at Victor's stubbornness.

Victor felt like his whole world had been turned upside down. All his dreams of being a powerful, swift hunter were vanishing. Suddenly, he wheeled away from his mother, banking so hard he almost stalled, and flew toward home as fast as he could.

"I don't wanna be a vulture!" he whimpered through clenched teeth, or rather, beak. "I don't wanna be a vulture! I don't *wanna* be a vulture!"

Victor reached his nest and made an awkward landing, then sat in the bottom and cried until he thought his heart would break.

That evening the flock came home, all of them looking fat and well fed. Victor's mother asked him, "Would you like me to regurgitate something for you, dear?"

Victor said, "NO! I don't wanna be a vulture and eat rotten stuff!"

Uncle Vlad said, "C'mon, kid, lighten up! Don't you remember the joke?" At this remark all the vultures in the flock held their breath in anticipation.

"A vulture's getting on a plane carrying a dead opossum under his wing. The stewardess makes a face and says, 'Uh, sir, may I put that in the luggage compartment for you?' And the vulture says, 'No thanks, this is carrion!' Get it? *Carry on*?" Vlad and the other flock members, who had all heard this joke about nine million times, screeched and whooped with glee, slapping each other with their wings. Victor had heard the joke about a million times, and had never got it. Now he did, and it just made him more disgusted!

Victor went to bed hungry. He lay in the nest for a long time, thinking and thinking. He was determined not to be a vulture!

The next morning he woke up with a plan. Before the other flock members were ready to fly, Victor launched himself off the nest toward the sunrise.

"Victor! Where are you going?" his father yelled after him.

"I'm going HUNTING!" Victor yelled back.

"Oh my," said Mother, feeling very upset.

Grandpa Val hopped over next to Mother and said, "Don't worry, Victoria. This happens every once in a while. Victor just hasn't realized what an important part vultures play in the way nature works. I'm afraid his Uncle Vlad confused him with all those stories about raptor hunters. It put all the wrong ideas in his head. Your brother always was a bit of a numbskull. Now Victor's convinced raptors look down on us for being scavengers." Val scratched his nose, or rather his beak, with his long toe. "I'll tell you what. Let me go talk to a few birds I know. I'll bet we can convince Victor how important his niche is after all."

Mother sniffed and said, "Do you think so? I hate to see him so unhappy!"

"Leave it to me," said Grandpa Val.

In the meantime, Victor was spiraling high above the desert floor by himself. He was determined to hunt something and prove that he could be something besides a scavenger! He had watched Red-tailed Hawks dive after rabbits, and it looked easy. Now he watched with eagle eyes (*Great description*! thought Victor) for movement in the cactus and shrubs below.

There! A movement caught his attention. He spotted a Cottontail hopping across the ground. Victor folded his wings and dove after it just as he had seen the hawks do. The rabbit got bigger and bigger until it was within range of Victor's fierce attack! But just as he was extending his claws, the rabbit heard him coming and took off with a sudden, lightning-fast bound. Victor tried to bank after it like he had seen the hawks do, but his wings didn't respond! Hawks can maneuver as fast as a rabbit, but vultures aren't built to fly like that! Poor Victor flew full speed into a creosote bush with a crash and a flurry of feathers.

"Gosh darn it!" he yelled as he untangled himself from the bush.

Clearly this approach wasn't going to work. Victor sat and tried to think what to do. He obviously couldn't outmaneuver a rabbit. But he was determined not to give up. What about hunting something else?

Then Victor remembered the Peregrine Falcon he had seen from the nest one day, far off and high up in the mountain air. While he had watched, astonished, the falcon dove on a small bird thousands of feet below it. Faster and faster the falcon plunged, its wings folded in close to its body. It dove so fast (Mother later told him up to 200 miles per hour!) Victor could hardly follow it with his eyes. It knocked the little bird out of the sky in a cloud of feathers, then circled gracefully down to carry the meal off to its chicks in a nest on a sheer cliff. Wow!

That was it, Victor decided. He would be a falcon and hunt in the air with speed and surprise as his allies. He wouldn't have to maneuver at all!

Picking the last bits of creosote bush out of his wings, Victor launched himself into the air and began circling to gain altitude. Higher and higher he soared, higher than he had flown before, higher, if he had known it, than vultures ever flew! Far below and off in the distance he saw birds in his own flock circling, looking for their day's disgusting food—no doubt something run over by a passing car. *Hah!* thought Victor. *Let them eat road pizza!* This time he would show them.

Victor flew so high that the air became quite chilly, and he could look straight sideways at pine forests on the mountain slopes. He was definitely up where the falcons flew!

It didn't take long for Victor to spy a small bird flying along, worry-free, at least a couple of thousand feet below him. A perfect target for a falcon! Victor executed a rollover that would have done any Peregrine proud. He plummeted earthward.

Downward he plunged, the air whistling through his wings as he gathered speed, until it seemed like the ground was rushing at him as fast as he was diving at the ground! He tucked his wings in as tightly as he could, mimicking the falcon's "stoop," as Mother had called it, which allows it to dive at such incredible speeds.

Faster and faster Victor dove, shattering the speed record for vultures (if he had only known it)! If a policeman with a traffic radar gun had been standing below to gauge Victor's speed, his display would have read more than 100 miles per hour—and Victor would have been the first vulture in history to get a speeding ticket!

Faster still he plunged, as the small bird below grew from a pinprick to a pencil point in size. The air was now shrieking through Victor's wing feathers. He was having a harder and harder time keeping his wings folded in the correct aerodynamic posture. But still his speed increased.

But poor Victor! Just as vulture wings are not made for fast maneuvering after rabbits, neither are they made for high-speed dives. Falcon wings are slender to minimize drag; vulture wings are wide to maximize lift for soaring on thermals. Just as Victor was beginning to think his dive would be a success, he felt a tremendous vibration shaking his wings. Suddenly he could barely hold them in as the air pressure buffeted them horribly. His primary and secondary feathers, the biggest feathers on a bird's wings, began to disappear in his slipstream, yanked out one by one! Suddenly, Victor lost his stability and tumbled out of control at 110 miles per hour! Feathers flew everywhere and the breath was snatched from his lungs as he fought to regain control, cartwheeling toward the ground, which was now *much* too close!

At last Victor managed to straighten his wings and pull up out of the dive, barely missing the top of a saguaro. Exhausted, he dropped to the ground and hopped into the shade of a mesquite tree to rest. He was panting, and his plumage was in total disarray, making him look like a feather duster that got caught in a tornado.

Victor was very discouraged, and about ready to give up. He sat and preened himself, slowly putting his feathers back in their place (except for the missing ones). His plan to be a bird of prey just wasn't working. So far he had tried to act like a Red-tailed Hawk and a falcon, and both attempts had failed.

Then Victor remembered the Harris's Hawks. The *cooperative* Harris's Hawks.

How could he have been so dumb? He didn't need to maneuver fast or dive quickly if he had *help*. But, um, that was a problem. Where to get help?

Suddenly he had it. Victor launched into the air and flew high until he spotted his flock still circling far off to the north. He put on speed and flew to catch them, but instead of joining his mother he aimed for two young vultures he knew.

"Hi Vickie! Hi Virginia!" Victor said cheerfully.

"Hi Victor!" said Vickie.

"What on earth happened to your feathers?" said Virginia.

"Uh, nothing," said Victor. "Say, I really need your help with something. Would you both come with me for a little while?"

Vickie and Virginia looked at each other skeptically. Both of them were ready to say "no"—after all, everyone in the flock knew Victor was a bit odd. But both of them also thought secretly that Victor was kind of cute.

"Where are we going?" said Vickie.

"Just follow me!" said Victor, and off he went, with Vickie and Virginia trailing behind, giggling and whispering to each other that Victor still looked cute even with a bunch of missing feathers.

Soon they were circling over a patch of what looked like promising rabbit habitat, and Victor explained his plan: "We're going to hunt cooperatively, just like the Harris's Hawks. When we see a rabbit we're all going to dive on it from different directions so it can't get away, and then we'll have a fresh meal and share it!"

Vickie and Virginia looked at each other for a moment. Then they said at the same time, "As *if*."

Victor said, "No, really! It will work! I've seen the Harris's Hawks do it. C'mon, we can do it, too!" Vickie and Virginia clearly thought this plan was crazy, but they were both slightly crazy about Victor, too, so they reluctantly agreed.

"Great!" said Victor, who started examining the ground below. Soon he saw what he was looking for. "Okay, right there between those two trees. See the rabbit? I'll come at it from behind, and you two dive from the left and the right. It can't get away!"

Still looking at each other skeptically, Vickie and Virginia wheeled away to their posts. When he saw they were in position, Victor nodded his head, and the three vultures dove out of the sky toward the rabbit, which froze when it saw several shadows coming toward it.

This will be easy, thought Victor.

And then, just as the three vultures attained top speed in their dives and were converging on the rabbit, it gave a huge kick with its hind legs and bolted away. All three vultures tried to bank at the last second, but we already know what happens when vultures try to maneuver too quickly. Victor, Virginia, and Vickie collided head-on in a huge cloud of feathers!

The three birds sat there rather dazed, Victor looking sheepish, Virginia and Vickie looking *mad*. "Uh . . . oops," said Victor.

"Yeah, oops is right!" said Vickie.

"Victor, this was your stupid idea!" said Virginia. "We should have known better than to listen to you, Mr. I'm-a-hunter."

"Yeah," teased Vickie. "*I'm a bird of prey, see my talons rip flesh*!"

"We're telling your mother," finished Virginia, and away the two vultures flew to do just that.

"Oh my," said Mother when she heard the story. In the meantime, poor Victor had flown to a far-off cliff and was sitting on a ledge, looking out over the desert. In the distance he could see a Red-tailed Hawk soaring high on a thermal. He was miserable. He knew now that he could never be a *real* raptor. No matter what he tried, it didn't work. Why, oh why, did he have to be hatched as a turkey vulture and not a falcon? What use was a bird that did nothing but eat dead stuff?

Victor stayed on the ledge and watched as the sun slowly sank into the hills.

It was well after dark when he silently flew back to his own nest ledge and settled down among the already sleeping members of the flock he wished wasn't his.

That night Victor had a nightmare. At first it seemed like a great dream: He and all the other vultures had been transformed into hawks and falcons, and were chasing after live rabbits and quail, making spectacular swoops and dives and yelling with the thrill of it.

But something went horribly wrong. The leftovers of the rabbits and rodents and birds and all the other things the former vultures caught started to pile up and stink awfully. The smell of one mostly eaten dead animal, Victor found in his nightmare, was *nothing* like the smell of about ten zillion mostly eaten dead animals that just stayed there on the ground, stinking worse and worse. And since the only things left to feed on the remains were maggots, which eventually turned into flies, the air was soon filled with billions and billions of flies, which tortured all the animals and got into their eyes and ears and noses. Victor dreamed he was a ferocious raptor all right, but a raptor covered with flies and barely able to breathe because of the stench that blanketed the whole world!

Victor woke up from his nightmare with a gasp and looked around in bright morning light, almost—*almost*—relieved to find he was still a vulture.

And then he thought he was still dreaming. Because when he looked beyond the ledge, none of the flock members was there. Instead, to Victor's astonishment, on a nearby rock stood two Red-tailed Hawks! And on a saguaro cactus nearby were three beautiful Harris's Hawks, and on top of the saguaro was a magnificent Peregrine Falcon! What the heck was going on?

"Good morning, Victor," said one of the Red-tails, "My name is Roger." "And I'm Regina," said the other Red-tail. "We're Hugo, Harriet, and Hilda," said one of the Harris's Hawks.

"How do you do, Victor," said the Peregrine, formally. "Allow me to introduce myself. My name is Percival."

"Um, uh . . . how do you do?!" Victor said formally, if a bit awkwardly, to all of them at once. He was terribly self-conscious, breathlessly admiring the fine plumage of the raptors and their fine, sleek heads, all the while thinking of his own featherless head and drab black feathers. He had no idea why these birds were here, but Victor wished *he* wasn't.

Then the Peregrine Falcon said, "We've come to thank you."

Victor stared at him. Had he heard that right?

One of the Red-tails said, "Yes, we predators rarely have the opportunity to express our appreciation for the vital role you scavengers play in the world."

"We never forget how important your job is, and we make sure we tell our fledglings, so they know it, too."

Victor couldn't believe his ears. The raptors were telling him how grateful they were to have vultures around!

The Harris's Hawk who Victor thought might be Hilda said, "Well, I appreciate the job you do, too, but I have to tell you, I always get a thrill watching how effortlessly you vultures soar on thermals. It's magnificent!"

Um . . . magnificent? thought Victor. Had she just described vultures as *magnificent*?

"I concur," said Percival. Victor wasn't sure what "concur" meant, but the falcon was nodding his head, so Victor supposed it meant, "Me, too." Wow.

"Anyway," said Roger, "We don't want to keep you from your job, so we'll be going. Give our best to the rest of your flock." And with a swish all six raptors flew off into the morning air.

Victor sat on the ledge, stunned. He felt as if his entire life had just been turned around *again*. All this time he had been admiring hawks and falcons and wishing he was one, and all the time those raptors admired him! They knew, as Victor was beginning to realize, that you didn't have to be a strong and swift hunter to have an important place in nature. And even if you had a funny-looking bald red head, you could still soar magnificently on thermals while hawks and falcons watched in admiration.

Slowly Victor stood up straighter. He rattled his wings to settle his primary feathers in perfect order. He looked out over the desert with new eyes.

"Well," said Victor the Vulture, "time to get to work." And he launched himself off the ledge and into the air, circling quickly to gain altitude.

In no time he was patrolling over a lonely two-lane road, and soon he spotted a rabbit lying on the side of the pavement.

"Hmm, that needs to be cleaned up," said Victor aloud, with a newfound sense of duty and pride.

The smell reached Victor, but, strangely, this time it didn't seem . . . too bad. In fact, it wasn't bad at all—not like something rotten, more like something . . . *aged*. Yes, that was it. It was a *mature* aroma, with finish notes of juicy, squirming maggot and a delicate overtone of putrefaction.

Victor spiraled gracefully and hungrily downward, licking his lips in anticipation.

Or rather, his beak.

Wildlife in the Story of Victor

Turkey Vulture
(Cathartes aura)

The common name "vulture" is used to describe birds that are found in many parts of the world. The vultures in North America and South America are not in the same family as the vultures in Africa, Europe, and Asia, but since they all feed on carrion, they are all called vultures. There are black vultures and white-backed vultures (and white-rumped vultures!), Egyptian vultures, Himalayan vultures, and lots more.

Turkey vultures like Victor are found in the United States, Mexico, and all over Central and South America. Can you guess why they are called turkey vultures? Look at pictures of wild turkeys. See that funny red head on the males? It looks a lot like a turkey vulture's red head, doesn't it? All vultures have either very tiny feathers or no feathers at all on their heads. This helps them stay clean when they are feeding, which helps them stay healthy.

Turkey vultures can be found as far north as Canada during the summer, but most of them north of the Mexican border migrate south for the winter. Only in some states in the Southeast and far South can you see turkey vultures all year. Some turkey vultures in the West migrate thousands of miles each fall, all the way to South America.

Turkey vultures nest in lots of different places, including old nests made by other birds, but they don't build their own. They really like ledges or little caves high up on cliffs. Once a vulture pair finds a nest site they like, they might use it for many years. The mother lays one, two, or three eggs, which hatch after about a month. The young birds stay with their parents for two or three months, until they can find food on their own. Then they become full-fledged members of a flock, which can have more than 20 birds. If you think that's a lot, you might be surprised to know that when turkey vultures gather to migrate there can sometimes be over a hundred in one group!

As the story of Victor makes clear, we're very lucky to have turkey vultures to take care of what would otherwise become mounds of rotten meat. Although other, usually smaller, creatures such as flies, beetles, worms, and bacteria play a role in recycling dead animals, forensic studies in Texas have shown that vultures are particularly quick and efficient at the task. They do a yeoman's job!

Red-tailed Hawk
(Buteo jamaicensis)

No matter where you live in the United States (except for Hawaii, way out in the ocean), you can see Red-tailed Hawks. They fly as far north as Alaska in the summer. Red-tailed Hawks are found in so many places because they are very good at hunting rodents, rabbits, and other common small mammals, and also some birds and reptiles. They will even eat rattlesnakes! One reason they are good at hunting is because their eyes are very sharp. A Red-tailed Hawk can spot a mouse eight times farther away than you or I can. (If you can spot a mouse 50 feet away, a red-tailed hawk could spot it about 400 feet away—clear across a football field and farther!)

Red-tailed Hawks build big nests of sticks in trees, on cliff ledges, or in saguaro cactuses in the southwestern United States. They will often use the same nest year after year, adding fresh sticks on top. A nest that has been used for many years can be up to six feet tall! Great Horned Owls, which don't build their own nests, often use old Red-tailed Hawk nests to lay their own eggs, and when that happens the hawk has to build a new nest. But you can find Great Horned Owl nests and Red-tailed Hawk nests in the same area, because the hawks hunt during the day and the owls hunt at night, so they don't compete for the same prey.

Harris's Hawk
(Parabuteo unicinctus)

Harris's Hawks are very beautiful birds. They are dark brown with copper on their shoulders and brilliant white bands on their tails. In the United States they are found only in the far Southwest, in states such as Texas and Arizona. Harris's Hawks are known for their cooperative hunting—that is, unlike other hawks in the United States, they typically hunt together. One or two (or sometimes three) young birds will often stay with their parents for an extra year or more, helping them hunt even after the parents have laid new eggs and are raising new hatchlings. When three or more birds help each other hunt, the odds of success are higher, and the young birds get extra experience before leaving to start their own families.

Harris's Hawks are big birds, and like most raptors, the females are larger than the males. But like all birds, they are very light for their size. Even a big Harris's Hawk will weigh less than three pounds; a dog that size could weigh thirty pounds.

Peregrine Falcon
(Falco peregrinus)

Peregrine Falcons are famous for being the fastest animals in the world. They can dive at speeds over 200 miles per hour, and even when just flying in a straight line above the ground they can go as fast as your family does in a car on the freeway! The word "peregrine" means "wanderer," and, boy, do Peregrines wander; some of them fly as far as 15,000 miles a year migrating from Canada all the way to South America. They also live almost everywhere. You can find Peregrine Falcons on every continent except Antarctica—even on a lot of islands in the ocean.

Peregrine Falcons commonly nest on ledges on cliffs, but they also like bridges and tall buildings in cities. Sometimes office workers on the fiftieth floor of a skyscraper can look out and see a Peregrine nesting right there on the window ledge! However, Peregrines don't build regular stick nests, so the female just lays three or four eggs right on the ledge. Hopefully, Peregrine hatchlings aren't afraid of heights!

California Leaf-nosed Bat
(Macrotus californicus)

When you first see a picture of a Leaf-nosed Bat, you might notice that its nose does look kind of like a leaf—but first you'll probably notice those huge ears! Leaf-nosed Bats can actually hear the tiny sounds an insect makes when it's walking; that's how good those gigantic ears are.

Like most other bats, Leaf-nosed Bats use sonar to catch insects when it's pitch dark, but this particular bat has large eyes and keen night vision, and even in the faintest light it prefers to use its eyes. When it uses its sonar, the bat makes very high-pitched sounds that people cannot here. But it can hear the echo of that sound as it bounces off the insect. The sonar is so good that a bat can fly through a thick dark forest or into a cave (where they sleep during the day), without ever running into anything.

Even though they can fly, bats are not birds; they are mammals just like us. They look sort of like mice with wings, but they are not closely related to mice, and they live a lot longer. A mouse might live for two or three years, but a Leaf-nosed Bat can live for 30 years!

Saguaro
(Carnegiea gigantea)

Saguaros (say *sa-wah-rose*) are some of the biggest cactuses in the world. They can be fifty feet tall or more. That's as tall as a five-story building. But they grow so slowly that a saguaro ten years old might be only two inches high! It can take them one hundred and fifty years to grow to their full height. Since they are often the tallest plants around, offering a great view from the top, you can sometimes see Red-tailed Hawks or Harris's Hawks perched on them, watching for prey. Saguaros have branches that look like arms waving at you, and hawks like to build nests on those arms. You might think having arms means saguaros are good to hug, but don't do it. They have sharp spines.

Saguaro roots grow close to the surface of the ground in a wide area around the main stem, so they can suck up a lot of water when it rains in the desert, which isn't very often. They store all that water in their thick green trunk and arms, which have pleats like an accordion so they can expand to hold hundreds of gallons of water. They get "fatter" with water after good rains and use the stored water during dry months. If you could see inside a saguaro's trunk, it would look like a very wet sponge.

Some kinds of woodpeckers peck holes in saguaros to build nests inside. The saguaro grows a hard lining on the walls of the hole, so the space inside the hole stays dry and comfortable for the birds. It stays much cooler in the nest cavity than outside because of all that moist cactus around it. When the woodpeckers move somewhere else, many other kinds of birds nest in their holes. When a saguaro finally dies and topples over, it is consumed by microbes and insects until you can easily see the woody ribs that held up the saguaro, and sometimes you'll find the hard linings of the nest cavities too. They often look a bit like shoes, so we call them "saguaro boots."

In the spring, saguaros grow pretty white flowers on top of their arms. After the flowers are pollinated (mainly by bats at night, or White-winged Doves and bees during the day) they turn into sweet red fruits. American Indians collected the fruits for food by using a long stick with a little stick tied on the end, like a hook, to pull them off.

Desert Cottontail
(Sylvilagus audubonii)

You can probably guess why this cute little rabbit is called a cottontail; its tail looks just like a fluffy white cotton ball. When the Desert Cottontail flashes that white tail, it warns nearby rabbits of danger nearby. You might think these tails would alert predators as well, but when a rabbit wants to hide, it simply sits very still with its tail down. When it does that, it looks just like the dirt and bushes around it, all soft brown or tan. And if a Desert Cottontail needs to run, it can do so at up to 20 miles per hour, zigzagging so fast you can hardly follow it with your eyes, much less your feet!

A female Cottontail gives birth to four or five kits (baby rabbits) at a time, in a soft nest she lines with fur from her own belly. The kits grow very fast, and Cottontails can have up to four or five litters per year, so that's a lot of Cottontail rabbits. But there are plenty of animals—such as coyotes, hawks, and bobcats—that prey on rabbits, so they keep the rabbit population under control. Otherwise, there would be rabbits everywhere, and they'd have no grass (their favorite food) left to eat!

Speaking of food, rabbits have strange table manners that seem pretty gross at first! Grass is very hard to digest, and when a Cottontail poops out little round pellets after eating grass, there's still a lot of nutrition in them. So it eats those first pellets again to digest them completely. When the pellets come out the second time, they are just hard little things, and the rabbit has gotten all the vitamins and minerals it needs! So be glad *you* don't have to eat grass.

Pinacate Beetle
(*Eliodes* spp.)

You might see this big black beetle walking across the desert some morning or evening. If you get very close you might see how it leaves tiny footprints like two lines of dots. Count the legs. It has six, just like all insects. Watch it, though—if the beetle sticks its rear end up in the air, back off! It can release a stink that drives off people and the animals that might try to eat the beetle. Believe it or not, a mouse called the grasshopper mouse eats Pinacate Beetles anyway. This mouse just sticks the back end of the beetle into the ground and eats the other end!

Pinacate Beetles have shiny, hard exoskeletons that look like a shell, which helps protect them. Under the shell they have wings, but the wings are tiny, and Pinacate Beetles never fly. In the wild, they eat tiny bits of grass and other plant materials.

Side-blotched Lizard
(*Uta stansburiana*)

A lot of animals are named for a mark or color you can easily see on them, like the Desert Cottontail or Red-headed Woodpecker or White-tailed Deer. So what can you guess about a Side-blotched Lizard? That's right; if you look closely, you can usually see a little black or dark blue blotch just behind each front leg.

Side-blotched lizards are very common in deserts all over the western United States. So if you are hiking, you have a good chance of spotting one, even though they are only about six inches long. When you see one on a rock, it might look like it's doing pushups. But it isn't exercising! It's letting other lizards know that that is *his* rock. The pushups say "Beat it!" to other lizards.

Side-blotched Lizards usually eat insects, but sometimes they eat things as big as scorpions. The females start laying eggs each year in spring. They can lay up to 12 eggs at a time, and can lay three clutches (a batch of eggs) every year.

Glossary

aerodynamic: A word used to describe a design that allows air or gases to flow easily around an object or a body. A smooth texture and fewer projections from the surface of an object creates less resistance to the flow of air and makes the object more aerodynamic.

altitude: A bird's altitude is its height above the ground. However, airplane pilots usually refer to their altitude as height above sea level. So if a plane is at an altitude of 20,000 feet above sea level, but flying over a 19,000-foot-tall mountain, its altitude above the ground is only 1,000 feet!

bank (in flight): Birds and airplanes both turn, or "bank," by tilting their wings, which changes the air pressure underneath to push them in the new direction.

carrion: A dead animal that can be eaten by scavengers.

drag: The resistance caused by air (or water) when something tries to move through it. If you've ever put your hand out the window of a car on the highway, you've felt drag as the air pushes against your hand. Airplanes and birds are streamlined so they encounter less drag when flying fast.

fledgling: A young bird that has grown its flight feathers but is still dependent on its parents.

hatchling: A baby bird that cannot yet fly.

maggot: The legless, soft-bodied larva of certain flies commonly found in decaying material.

maneuver (verb): To move with skill and care, usually for a specific purpose.

niche: The role that an animal or other living thing fills in nature. A turkey vulture's niche is to clean up dead animals. A red-tailed hawk's niche is to help control the rodent and rabbit population.

plumage: A general term for all the feathers on a bird.

preen: Smooth or clean feathers with the beak or tongue.

prey (noun): An animal taken by another animal as food; (verb) to take an animal for food.

primary feathers: The biggest feathers a bird has on its wings, out at the tips; secondary feathers are the next biggest, in the middle of the wing; tertials are the wing feathers right next to the body.

putrefaction: One of the stages of a decomposing animal or the process by which a dead animal decays due to the action of tiny bacteria or other microbes or organisms inside it.

raptor: A general term for birds such as hawks, eagles, falcons, and owls. Raptors are generally defined as "birds of prey"— those that hunt and eat other animals— especially those that use their feet (talons) to hunt. Until recently vultures and condors, who are primarily carrion eaters, were listed as raptors by most birding authorities. Now, most scientists believe turkey vultures are more closely related to storks, with which they share key physical characteristics and behaviors. No wonder Victor was confused.

rollover: When a bird of prey, such as a falcon, needs to dive suddenly, it rolls completely over on its back and plunges straight down. This is a rollover. Fighter airplanes can do this too.

scavenger: An animal that eats carrion.

stall (in flight): If a bird or airplane tries to fly too slowly or turn too quickly, the air under its wings can no longer support it, and it will fall instead of fly. This is stalling.

stoop: The speedy dive of a falcon, for which it tucks its wings tightly against its body to minimize drag.

thermal: When a spot on the ground, such as a dark paved road or a bunch of black rocks, absorbs extra heat from the sun, the air above it is heated too. Since hot air is less dense than cool air, the heated air rises in a column, creating what we call a thermal.

updraft: The movement of air upward, such as the rising air in a thermal.

The Desert Museum gratefully acknowledges our clear-thinking and sharp-eyed proofers for the English and Spanish editions— Susan Campbell and Jesús García, respectively—and all those who worked behind the scenes to make this book a reality. We are also indebted to Amadeo Rea and Gary Nabhan for their generous reviews.

Acknowledgments

First, thanks to my wife, Roseann. We are closing in on 30 years of exploring together, and as Uncle Chamma said, she's still "just the right size to hug." Also Bruce Douglas, Huck to my Tom, or was it the other way around? I'm really happy we weren't squished by that prickly-pear-shingled lean-to. Kim Duffek apparently accomplished some sort of long-distance mind meld; I couldn't have imagined more perfect illustrations of how Victor played out in my head. And thank you, Linda Brewer, for the fastest "Yes" to a manuscript in publishing history, and for thoughtful editing that did just what editing is supposed to do: make a better book.

Jonathan Hanson ~ Tucson, Arizona

I am indebted to Linda Brewer and Arch Brown, who worked so hard to make me a part of this book project, and to Jonathan Hanson for finding the words for such an engaging tale. Thanks also to George Montgomery and Maureen Bicknase, and to all the dedicated staff at the Desert Museum who inspire me every day. My heartfelt gratitude goes to family and friends who nurture and support the work I do. Lastly, I would very much like to thank my reluctant model, Flo, the Turkey Vulture, and her keepers. Without them, my job of illustrating this book would have been much more difficult.

Kim Kanoa Duffek ~ Tucson, Arizona

About the Author

Jonathan Hanson grew up exploring the Sonoran Desert outside Tucson, Arizona, and has since explored other deserts from the Namib to the Sahara. He and his friend Bruce once played dead to see if they could trick some circling vultures into landing near them, but they only succeeded in alarming a passing motorist, who was shocked to see two boys lying motionless by the side of the road.

Jonathan and his wife, Roseann, have written several natural history books together, including the *Southern Arizona Nature Almanac* and *50 Common Reptiles and Amphibians of the Southwest*. They live in a tiny solar and wind-powered cottage in the middle of the Sonoran Desert. They count among their neighbors coyotes, deer, mountain lions, foxes, and lots of birds—including, of course, turkey vultures.

Photo by Gary Haynes

About the Illustrator

Kim Duffek's interest in art and nature began at a young age. When she wandered home from a day of playing in the Midwestern tallgrass prairie, where she grew up, her mother would often put a paintbrush in her hand. As an adult she earned degrees in both wildlife ecology and studio art, and she continues to be passionate about art and nature. Currently she works in the botany department at the Arizona-Sonora Desert Museum, pursuing wildlife art as her other career. She is also a member of a musical canine freestyle club that hosts public dog-dancing performances.